3011205(

GW00360248

Ladybird Readers

Pablo Chooses His Shoes

Series Editor: Sorrel Pitts
Text adapted by Hazel Geatches
Song lyrics by Wardour Studios

LADYBIRD BOOKS

UK | USA | Canada | Ireland | Australia
India | New Zealand | South Africa

Ladybird Books is part of the Penguin Random House group of companies
whose addresses can be found at global.penguinrandomhouse.com.
www.penguin.co.uk   www.puffin.co.uk   www.ladybird.co.uk

Penguin
Random House
UK

Text adapted from *Pablo Picks His Shoes* by Andrew Brenner and Sumita Majumdar,
first published by Ladybird Books Ltd, 2020
Based on the *Pablo* TV series created by Gráinne Mc Guinness
This Ladybird Readers edition published 2022
001

Text and illustrations copyright © Paper Owl Creative, 2021
Pablo copyright © Paper Owl Creative, 2015

PAPER OWL FILMS

Printed in China

A CIP catalogue record for this book is available from the British Library

ISBN: 978-0-241-53374-1

All correspondence to:
Ladybird Books
Penguin Random House Children's
One Embassy Gardens, 8 Viaduct Gardens, London SW11 7BW

MIX
Paper from
responsible sources
FSC® C018179

Ladybird Readers

Pablo Chooses His Shoes

Based on the *Pablo* TV series
Original story by Rosie King

Picture words

Pablo

Tang

Wren

Draff

Llama

Mouse

Noa

shoes

trainers

sandals

boots

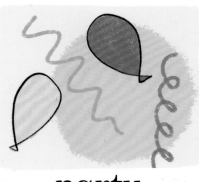

party

Pablo is going to Granny's house today.

"Can we go, too?"
ask the friends.

"Yes!" says Pablo.

"Can we go, too?" ask Pablo's blue shoes.

"They can go on your feet!"
says Draff.

"Can we go, too?" ask Pablo's yellow trainers.

"Can we go, too?" ask Pablo's orange sandals.

"I'm sorry," says Pablo.
"I cannot choose."

"Your friends can wear us,"
say the yellow trainers.

The yellow trainers are too big for Wren!

The orange sandals are too small for Noa!

"Choose us, Pablo!" say all
the shoes.

"I'm sorry," says Pablo.
"I cannot choose."

"You can wear shoes on your hands!" says Tang.

Pablo wears shoes on his
hands and his feet . . . and
his head!

Then Pablo's brown shoes
and his purple boots say,
"Can we go, too?"

Pablo is sad.

He runs from his shoes.

"I'm sorry," says Pablo.
"I cannot choose."

"I can choose," says Draff.
"Wear the blue shoes today."

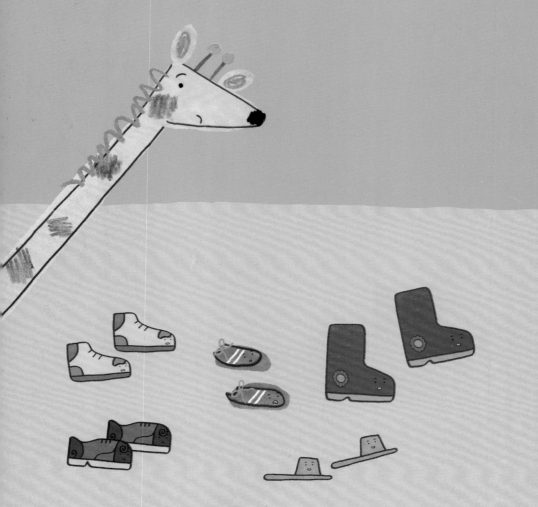

Pablo wears the blue shoes
and goes to Granny's house.
He is happy.

The yellow trainers, the orange sandals, the brown shoes, and the purple boots all have a party at Pablo's house. They are happy, too!

Activities

The key below describes the skills practiced in each activity.

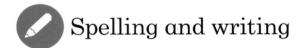 Spelling and writing

 Reading

Speaking

Listening*

Critical thinking

Singing*

Preparation for the Cambridge Young Learners exams

*To complete these activities, listen to the audio downloads available at **www.ladybirdeducation.co.uk**

1 Find the words. 📖

shoes
sandals
trainers
party

trishoesmkusandalstidntrainersofcndpartyobirk

2 **Read the sentences and match them with the correct picture. Write 1—4.**

1 These are blue shoes.

2 These are orange sandals.

3 These are yellow trainers.

4 These are purple boots.

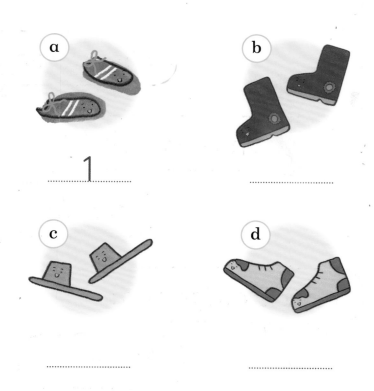

a

____1____

b

....

c

....

d

....

3 Work with a friend.
Talk about the picture. 💬 ✦

1 Who is this?

This is Tang.

2 Is he an animal?

Yes, he . . .

3 What color is he?

He is . . .

4 Put a ✓ by the things you see in Pablo's bedroom. 📖

1	bag	✓	**2**	banana	☐
3	bird	☐	**4**	book	☐
5	boots	☐	**6**	boy	
7	girl	☐	**8**	hat	☐
9	jacket	☐	**10**	sandals	☐
11	bed	☐	**12**	T-shirt	☐
13	trainers	☐	**14**	trousers	☐

5 **Look at the picture and read the questions. Write one-word answers.**

1 Where is Pablo going?

To Granny's .... house ....

2 Can his friends go? ....

3 Who wants to go, too?

His blue ....

6 **Complete the sentences.**
Write a—d.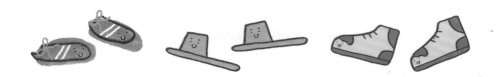

1 Can we   b

2 They can go   ....

3 I'm sorry—   ....

4 Your friends   ....

a can wear us.

b go, too?

c I cannot choose.

d on your feet!

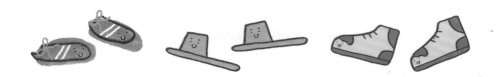

7 **Who says this?**

Draff   the trainers   Pablo   Tang

1 "They can go on your feet!"

says _____Draff_____.

2 "I'm sorry. I cannot choose,"

says _____.

3 "Your friends can wear us!"

say _____.

4 "You can wear shoes on
your hands!"

says _____.

8 **Listen, and write the answers.**

1 Where does Pablo wear the yellow trainers?

on his hands

2 Where does Pablo wear the blue shoes?

3 What does he wear on his head?

4 What do the brown shoes and the purple boots say?

5 Pablo is sad. What does he do?

9 Choose the correct words and write them on the lines.

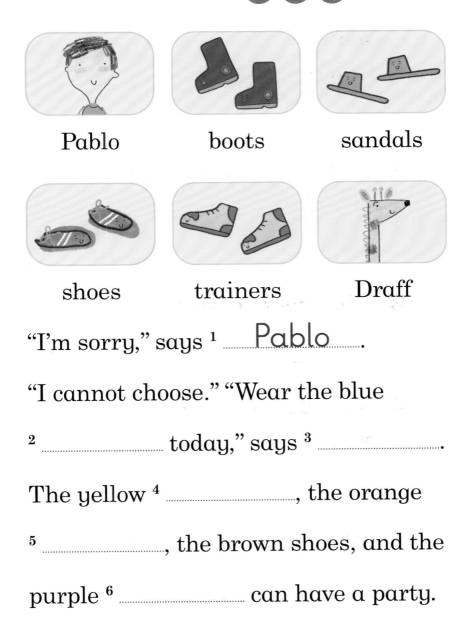

Pablo   boots   sandals

shoes   trainers   Draff

"I'm sorry," says [1] ___Pablo___.

"I cannot choose." "Wear the blue

[2] _____ today," says [3] _____.

The yellow [4] _____, the orange

[5] _____, the brown shoes, and the

purple [6] _____ can have a party.

10 **Look and read. Write *yes* or *no*.**

1 Pablo is at home.   no

2 Pablo is sad.

3 Pablo's shoes are at home.

4 They are having a party.

5 They are happy.

11 **Circle the correct words.**

1 Pablo wears the blue
   a boots.   **b** shoes.

2 He goes to Granny's
   a flat.   **b** house.

3 He is
   a happy.   **b** yellow.

4 The shoes at Pablo's house have
   a a party.   **b** dinner.

12 **Work with a friend. You are Pablo. Your friend is Pablo's shoes. Ask and answer the questions.**

Can I go to Granny's house, too?

Yes, you can.

Can you wear me on your head?

Can you wear me on your feet?

13 **Look and read. Write *can* or *cannot*.**

1 " _____ Can _____ we go, too?" ask
Pablo's yellow trainers.

2 "I'm sorry," says Pablo.
"I _____ choose."

3 "Your friends _____ wear us,"
say the yellow trainers.

4 Pablo _____ choose.
He is sad.

14 **Write _small_, _big_, _happy_, or _sad_.**

1 They are too
_____big_____!

2 The orange sandals are too
_____ for Noa!

3 Pablo cannot choose.
He is _____.

4 Pablo wears the blue shoes.
He is _____.

5 The shoes have a party.
They are _____, too!

15 **Write the correct sentences.**

1 can   feet   go   on   They   !   your

They can go on your feet!

2 can   friends   us   wear   !   Your

....

3 The   trainers   big   are   Wren   yellow   too   for   .

....

4 are   for   Noa   orange   !   sandals   small   The   too

....

16 Do the crossword.

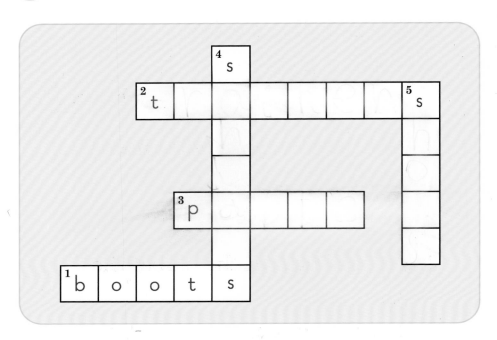

Across

1 They are purple.

2 They are too big for Wren!

3 The shoes are happy because they have a . . .

Down

4 They are orange.

5 Pablo cannot choose his . . .

17 Circle the correct answers.

1 Where is Pablo going?

   a He is going to a party.

   b He is going to Granny's house.

2 What shoes does Pablo choose?

   a His blue shoes.

   b His purple boots.

3 How is Pablo at the end of the story?

   a He is happy.

   b He is sad.

18 **Order the story. Write 1—4.**

.... Pablo cannot choose his shoes.

......1...... Pablo is going to Granny's house.

.... Pablo's shoes have a party.

.... Pablo wears the blue shoes.

Pablo is going to Granny's house.
The shoes ask, "Can we go, too?"
The trainers are too big!
The sandals are too small!
What will Pablo do?

The shoes say, "Choose us, Pablo!"
Pablo is sad. He cannot choose.
The purple boots say, "Choose us!" too.
Pablo runs from the shoes.

Pablo goes to Granny's house.
He is happy. His shoes are blue.
The shoes at Pablo's house have a party.
They are happy, too!

Visit www.ladybirdeducation.co.uk
for more FREE Ladybird Readers resources

✓ Digital edition of every title
✓ Audio tracks (US/UK)
✓ Answer keys
✓ Lesson plans

✓ Role-plays
✓ Classroom display material
✓ Flashcards
✓ User guides

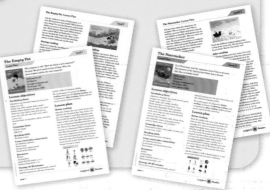

Register and sign up to the newsletter to receive your FREE classroom resource pack!

To access the audio and digital versions of this book:

1 Go to www.ladybirdeducation.co.uk
2 Click "Unlock book"
3 Enter the code below

tj26RLuBUo